CONTROL
ROOM

Please visit our website, www.west44books.com.
For a free color catalog of all our high-quality books,
call toll free 1-800-542-2595 or fax 1-877-542-2596.

**Cataloging-in-Publication Data**

Names: Wolf, Ryan.
Title: Control room / Ryan Wolf.
Description: New York : West 44, 2021. | Series: West 44 YA verse
Identifiers: ISBN 9781538385203 (pbk.) | ISBN 9781538385210
  (library bound) | ISBN 9781538385227 (ebook)
Subjects: LCSH: Children's poetry, American. | Children's poetry,
  English. | English poetry.
Classification: LCC PS586.3 C668 2021 | DDC 811'.60809282--dc23

First Edition

Published in 2021 by
Enslow Publishing LLC
101 West 23rd Street, Suite #240
New York, NY 10011

Editor: Caitie McAneney
Designer: Seth Hughes

Photo Credits: Cover (eye) Minutius Hora/Shutterstock.com; cover
(texture) Ana Babii/Shutterstock.com; cover (lens flare) NJ Design/
Shutterstock.com.

Printed in the United States of America

CPSIA compliance information: Batch #CW20W44: For further information contact
Enslow Publishing LLC, New York, New York at 1-800-542-2595.

*For Mick Cochrane,*
*a genuine guide.*

*Special thanks*
*to my family*
*and to Joshua Davidson,*
*Caitie McAneney,*
*Thomas Morrison,*
*and Ian Richardson*
*for their spirited support.*

# HELIORAS WELCOMES YOU!

An Introduction
to the Present Moment

# GROWTH

When he switches on
the lights,
my eyelids
snap
down.
Block out
the sudden white.

I hold myself
    inside
the bright red
behind my lids.
Then blink
the room
into focus.

"How are you feeling,
Maggie?"
    Terrance asks
    with too much
    sweetness.
"Are you well?
I feel
just terrible
about bringing you here
last night.

This was only
    a misunderstanding."

I won't say
anything.
I'm a child
tossed
in time out.

I won't give
adult answers
to a man who isn't
        my father.

Terrance leans in
to touch
my forehead.
His blond bangs
        hang
        over me.

"Your energy is low,"
        he says
        with his usual calm.
"But I don't judge you.
        Or think
        any less of you.

You don't think
        less of a seed
        because it isn't
                a tree.

I know
the love inside you
        will grow."

I won't say
anything.
Terrance tells us
life is only
where you place
your attention.

I want to
        throw it
                far away
                        from here.

Into a melting memory.
A family vacation
when Dad was alive.
A morning bike ride
on a summer road.

Then maybe
        I won't be
        one more mind
        for Terrance's collection.

I try to
pull
up
memories
from my brain
        like weeds
        in the community garden.

Terrance's voice
        breaks through
        my thoughts.

"The pain
and punishment
of staying
in the Growth Room
is really a gift,"
        he says.
"Pain *is* growth,
in the body
and in the spirit.
And pain
is only
one stage.

        It's not
        the end.

It's not even
something
that lasts
        for very long.

We will get
to a better *now*
together.
Believe this."

I won't nod
and forgive.

        *I won't say*
        *anything.*
        *Won't say*
        *anything.*
        *Won't say* —

His hands
        cup
        my cheeks.

Terrance peers
into me.

His eyes
are like
        windows
        facing the sea.

He speaks
        even more slowly,
                even more gently.

"I know you
love your mum.
You sent that note
to the news
to protect her.

But you must
        move beyond
        your fear
        for her safety.

No one is safe
in the end,"
        he says.

        *I won't say*
        *anything.*

"I'm only here
to guide you,"
        he goes on.
"Further than
        your fears.

You can trust
the Helioras system.

It has worked.
And will continue
        to work.

            For your mum
            and for you."

My attention
        throws itself
                to thoughts
                of my mother.

Every piece of
hippie jewelry
she ever wore.
Promising
cosmic energies.
Bringing her
closer
to a
higher
state.

            *Are we close now?*
            *Are we close?*

I should've been
        the mother
        to my mother.

I should've never
        let her
        be charmed
        by men
        who promise
        more than forever.

I can't let him
keep me
locked
away
from her.

In her gray jumpsuit.

Tearing
out
her
hair.

        Hair going gray.

                Mind going gray.

I can't hold
the words
in my chest
        any longer.

"I'm grateful
for your mercy, Terrance,"
        I lie
        to those
        seaside windows.
"I'll never
do it again."

"Never do what,
my spark of sunlight?"
        he asks
        with a kind grin.

"I promise
not to contact
any outside media,"
        I tell him.
"I won't send
        any emails or calls
        to anyone."

"That's beautiful,"
        he says
        with a smile.
"What you did
*was* hurtful, though.
Directing evil
toward
the people
who love you.

        What would
        you say
        to them
        now?"

"I'm sorry,"
        I cry.

        My palms
        are sweating.
        They heat
        the pattern
        of the sun
        formed by the
        floor tiles.

"It was only
a joke,"
        I say.
"I beg
the forgiveness
of my brothers
and sisters.

Your system
        is true.

Your punishments
        are gifts.

Please, *please*,
        let me out.

Let me
return."

# DISEASE

After Terrance
unlocks
the Growth Room,
I join the others
in the Enlightenment Hall.
The daily broadcast
will start soon.

They smile at me:
the men and women
in their gray jumpsuits.
Like I was
never even gone.

Even Mom smiles
through cracked lips.
She pats the mat
next to her
        and I sit.

She looks rested.
I don't know if
        I slept at all
        last night.

There was no sleeping bag
in the Growth Room.
Only cold tiles
in the darkness.

I cross my legs
and look around the hall.
Chinara Ogbu is
beside her father.
She's the only person
who doesn't smile
at me.

Her eyes are on
the carpet's
peacock design.

Terrance says
        the feathers
        of the peacock
        are the eyes
                of the stars.

There's a long
widescreen TV
in the back of
the Enlightenment Hall.
When it comes on,
        everyone
        cheers.

Terrance appears
on the screen.
Soothing music,
        overlaid with
        tinkling chimes,
        plays as he
        blows us
        a kiss.

"Good morning,
my sparks of sunlight,"
        he says.

He speaks with
a pleasant
Australian accent.

His hair
is so bright,
it almost glows.

"You are beautiful,"
he tells us.
"Every day
you get more and more
beautiful.

        The energy
        you give
        makes the world better.

        By thinking
        of light,
        you bring the world light.

        By thinking
        of peace,
        you bring the world peace.

        You save the world
        each day,
        just by
        being you."

Everyone snaps
their fingers
to celebrate this.
I do it
along with them,
> even if it hurts
> my thumbs.

"Now, yesterday
was disappointing,"
> Terrance continues
> without
> blinking.
"One of *you*
forgot
why we're here.
Forgot how important
positive thought
and energy is."

Everyone around me
> shakes
> their heads.

I shake my head
with them.

> Even though
> I am
> shaking
> my head
> at myself.

"A reporter
from Public Access
wanted to speak
with me,"
           Terrance says.
"About a message
she received
from one of *you*.
A message,
we now know,
was meant as a joke.

Now, some jokes
bring life.
This joke
was meant
to harm."

Everyone lowers
their heads,
frowning.

I frown too.

"There's a reason why
only *some* of you
have laptops and phones,"
           says Terrance.
"They're for work only.

Through work,
           you help
           build
           our community.

But electrical waves
in your devices
carry
distracting energies.

We always need
to guard our minds
        from evil.

By reading
and seeing
        evil things,
we poison
our minds.

Bad ideas
are like bad foods.

They make you
sick.

Many outside
these walls
        are sick.

They don't listen
to their hearts.
They listen
        to noise.

Their diseased thoughts
        form
        diseased minds."

"And can diseased minds
see the truth?"
          Terrance asks.

          The group
          shouts, NO!

"Can they possibly
          understand
          the wonderful thing
          we're doing here?"

NO!
          NO!

"The message
one of *you*
sent the media
called us
          a *cult*.

One of *you* stole
the laptop of
a hardworking member
of *our* group
to spread
a dangerous lie.

Do you know what
others will do
if they think
we're a *cult*?

They'll tear us
          to *p i e c e s.*

They'll take children
        away from
        their parents.
Throw us all
in filthy prisons."

        Terrance's voice is steady,
        but a single tear
        rolls
        from his right eye.

"The light is
so dim
in so many hearts.

They don't see
the good work
we do.

We're *not*
a cult.

We are a loving
        community of friends.
We are equality in a world
        that *hates*
        the poor and weak.
We are truth in a world
        that *loves*
        lies.
We are freedom in a country
        that doesn't know
        what freedom
        really is."

My mom
is weeping.
Crying much harder
        than Terrance.

She will not
face me now.

"We are free
        to love one another,"
        Terrance says,
        as the music rises
        behind him.
"We are free
        to follow the path
        to wholeness.
We are free
        to heal
        a broken universe."

The room erupts
with more cheers.
More snapping fingers.

I see Mark,
my mother's boyfriend,
        pumping his arms.
He's sitting up front
        next to Lila,
        Terrance's personal assistant.

Lila rubs Mark's shoulders
        and whistles
        at the screen.

"From now on,
I will be tracking
the internet use
of those
I *generously*
allowed
laptops and phones,"
        Terrance says.

The soothing music
is so loud
at this point,
        it's hard
        to hear him.

"This ensures
        none of you
        become poisoned
        by brainwashing ideas.

I don't want you
        seeing
        or spreading
        *evil.*

We need to
watch out
for each other.

We need to
        stay
        safe."

The music
        cuts out
as the face
on the screen
breathes in deeply.

"Peace and love
to you all
on this day
as it blooms.

        Remain in joy."

Terrance bows
his head.
The TV goes blank.
Everyone leaps
to hug one another.

Mom squeezes me,
        pressing her wet cheek
        against mine.

"I forgive you,"
        she says,
        her hair tangled
        in my own.
"You'll always be
        my spark of sunlight.
Just follow your
        mind's eye. Seek the light
        in your
        beautiful heart."

*Can't you see through this?*
        I want to
        scream
        into her curls.
*After what he did*
        *to you?*

*Just fifteen minutes ago,*
        *Terrance told me*
        *safety*
        *wasn't real.*
*Now he's digging in*
        *his claws*
        because of safety.

*He already*
*controls*
*what you wear*
        *and eat*
*and say*
        *and do.*

        What more
        can he take?

Before I can speak,
Mr. Ogbu comes by.
Gives me a bear hug.
Says he can forgive me
for using
his computer
        to send an evil email
                to evil people
                who'll only hurt us.

You'll slip
*away*
from everyone.

Leave them

        *forever.*

And *you have*
*no control*
*over this.*
No control
*at all.*

No matter
how strong
Dad was.
How many rivers
he kayaked
       across.
How many hills
he hiked
       up.
How much
he loved
       our family.
Loved this world.

       He still lost it.

We knew by then
he'd never
wake up.

I looked
harder
at the reflection
in the hospital window.

Mark stood
with my mom
      in the back
      of the room.

She had met Mark
two weeks
into Dad's coma.

He was
the lawyer who was
making sure
our family
"won every penny,
      nickel,
dime,
      quarter,
and fifty-cent
piece
we deserved."

He promised
to take
down
the "drunken animal"
      who'd
      hit
      Dad's motorcycle.

Mark was
our ally.
Providing
his legal services
        *pro bono:*
for free.

Through the window,
I saw him
rubbing
Mom's shoulders.

The same playful
rub
Lila would later
give to Mark
in the
Enlightenment Room.

The same
suggestive
        motions.

Here,
in front of Dad.
Who was
still living.
Even if he
was lost.
Tunneling
inside himself.

The lines
on the monitor
        wobbled
                on.

I knew
Mom
was hurting.

So she
let Mark
touch her.
Didn't
        flinch.

She even
        rubbed
        Mark's hand.

Her other fingers
grasped
a healing crystal
she wore
around
her neck.

They pinched
the pink quartz.

Her eyes
closed
tight.
As tight
as Dad's.

"You're the
strongest person
I know,"
      Mark whispered
      into Mom's
      neck.
"We're going
to find
      justice.
And you're going
to find
      peace.
Because
you deserve
      both."

I made myself
look straight
at Dad.
His skin
was scarred,
but warm.
I saw
the slow
      rhythm
of life
in his chest.
But he couldn't
get up
and scream
at Mark or Mom.

He was there,
      but not there.

"You're okay,"
            I heard Mark
            whisper.
"Someday,
you'll be
more than okay.
This will
            pass on.
It'll be
totally gone.
And you'll be
            in a better,
            more beautiful
            place.

Picture yourself
            in the future.
Maybe at
Stinson Beach.
            Lying on a blanket.
                        Drinking in
                        every
                        spark
                        of sunlight.

                        Everything that's
                        good
                        about this world."

*Wrong.*

All
            wrong.

Picture instead
the headlights
that swallowed
Dad's soul.

His helmet
cracked
on the pavement.
The trail
of blood,
pointing
like the red needle
of a compass
toward the
broken motorcycle.

The
broken
body.

"It's going to be okay,"
said Mark.
He touched
Mom's hand
where
it pinched
the crystal.

And that was the moment when
Dad's
vital signs
went                    flat.

# CHESS

Three weeks after
Dad's funeral,
I was driving
with Mom.
A misty rain
sprayed
our windshield
lightly.

She had
picked me up
from
Chess Club
after school.
There was
a tournament
scheduled
that month.

Chess was
a decent
distraction.

Focusing on
the fixed
board.

Living inside
its square
borders.

Pouring my
mind into my
next move.

Blocking off
the rest of
my thoughts.

Mom's phone
was plugged into
the car stereo.
She was listening
to a podcast.
The voice
of a man
from Australia.
This was the
third time
I'd heard her
listening
        to him.

"Your life
is where
you place
your attention,"
        the voice said,
        stretching
        each vowel.
"It's what you
choose to
give yourself to
        *now.*"

I thought of
my chess game.
How I gave
my mind to it.
What the voice said
made some sense.

The misty spray
of rain
turned into
solid droplets.
They reminded me
of Dad,
but I couldn't
think of why.

Mom was
        scrunching
her nose.

This meant
she was
listening
hard
to the speaker.

"You can't step
outside the *now*,"
        the voice
        went on.
"You just have to
make it
        the best *now*
        possible.
You do this
by giving your
attention
to what's
        most beautiful
        about
                *this*    moment."

And what
if you can't?
I thought.

       What if
       your brain
       won't
       let you?

       Because
       someone
       left it
           bleeding
               on a roadside.

The voice
seemed to
know my
thoughts.

"You are
not
your brain,"
       it said.
"You are part of
       an endless
       mind.

We are all
sparks
from the
same sun."

"So soak up
the rays within,"
　　　the voice
　　　cooed.
"You can
*always*
find
　　　waves
　　　　　　of positivity
　　　and joy.

They already
　　　*v i b r a t e*
　　　in your
　　　deepest
　　　self.

They want you
　　　to
　　　　　　*grow.*

Can you
*feel*
them
in
your
spine?

　　　They're there."

As the man
spoke,
I did feel
a *crackle*
in my
lower back.

"Did you
pick up
on that wonderful
energy?"
　　　the voice
　　　asked.
"Terrific,
　　　isn't it?

Our society sends
　　　so much noise.
　　　　　So much
　　　　　negativity.

But inside,
you can
　　　*turn off*
　　　*the evils*
　　　*of this world.*

Pay attention
to the light
rippling
　　　inside."

There was a
        flutter
in my stomach.
        It sped off
        quickly.

"Who is this?
He's putting me
to sleep,"
        I lied.

"It's Terrance David,"
        said Mom,
        turning
        down the
        volume.
"He speaks about
        science and
        spirituality.
His voice *is*
        quite the lullaby.

I haven't heard him
        say anything
        my heart
        doesn't
        already feel.

And he says it
        so *powerfully*."

"He sounds
pretty cheesy,"
        I said.

"That's because
your heart's
not ready
for his level
of awakening,"
        Mom argued.
"You're young.
Maybe you
should practice
improving
your *now*
by using your
        mind's eye."

My eyebrows
        rose with the
windshield wipers.

"When you picture
a beautiful future,
your positive thinking
creates
a beautiful *now*,"
        Mom explained.
"Mark taught me
that trick.
Come to find out,
he learned it
        from Terrance.
He actually goes to
meetings
with the guy
        we're listening to."

"So that's why
Mark sounds like
such a creep
all the time,"
          I said.

"Listen, Maggie."
          Mom scowled.
"Mark's an
amazing man.

He's done
a zillion things
for us.
No one's
ever been
kinder.
          More comforting.
                    More willing
                    to listen to me.

Most men
just *zone out*
when you try
to talk with them.

But Mark's always
so present."

"More than Dad
was?"
          I asked
          bitterly.

"I won't speak badly
of your father,"
        Mom said.
"He was
full of ... *zest*.
Loved a thrill.
And sometimes
        that pulled him
                away from us.

I miss him more
than you know.
But you and me —
        we don't deserve
        to be unhappy
        forever.

He wouldn't
want that."

Mom scrunched
her nose again.
Stared at
the wipers.

"Mark invited me to
a weekend retreat
at Terrance David's
Helioras Healing Center,"
        she said
        quietly.
"Mark's paying for me.
        I'm gonna
                go."

*Wrong.*

All
        wrong.

I watched the
wipers.
*Rising.*
        *Falling.*
                *Squeaking.*

I pictured a
chessboard grid
on the windshield.
Began making
        moves
        in my mind's eye.

"I'm tired of feeling
*shattered*
all the time,"
        Mom said,
        even more
        softly.
"I thought
these crystals
I bought
would help.
But they're not
        enough.

Terrance
*really*
helps people."

I slumped
        into
        my seat.

I didn't know it then,
but in 10 months,
        I would
        leave my
        home
        and high school.

Move 90 miles
        down
        the California coast.

All because of
how much
Terrance
helped
her.

But in that moment,
        that lost *now*,
I moved an
        imaginary knight
        in front of
        imaginary pawns.

And the wipers
        brushed
                the game
away.
Brushed away
                the flitting raindrops
                        of my thoughts.

# SERPENTS

It was
the middle
of my junior year.

Mom showed me
a hand-signed letter
on yellow paper.
I recognized
the logo
at the top
of the sheet.
A sun
with
two
winding
        snakes
    inside of its circle.

The message
said
we were
selected
for a special
Sun Sparks Team.
We needed to
leave our homes.
Move to the
Helioras Healing Center.
        In 30 days.

Terrance
was personally impressed
by Mom.
He told her
she was
filled with
focus.

She went to
to his retreats
every
month.

She attended
meetups
with Helioras members
every
week.

She listened to
Terrance's podcasts
every
day.

She did
the stretches
he'd invented
twice a day.

And practiced
his breathing exercises
every other
hour.

The letter said
she was
perfect for
a new movement
taking place.

It would bring
together
Helioras members
from all over
the world.

They would
live together
in a cleaner,
more peaceful
way.

They would
join energies
to send out
waves of light
to the rest of
humanity.

The Center would be
self-supporting.
Members could
leave the drain
of their current jobs.
Live out
fuller *nows*.

Mark called Mom.
Told her he was
also invited
to join
the Sun Sparks.

But if Mom and Mark
were leaving,
        I needed to go
        with them.

The Healing Center
had its own school.
Basically homeschooling.
But I could get
my diploma
there.

But this meant
no more
chess tournaments.
        No more
        cafeteria gossip.
                No more
                book talks
                and movie days.
                        No more
                        pasting pictures
                        in my locker
                        of Dad and me.
                                No more
                                walking the stage
                                with my friends
                                        at graduation.

"Public
schools
just teach you
hate and fear,
anyhow,"
        Mom said.

"That's not
true,"
        I argued.
"You *know*
that's not
        true."

"Maggie,
this is the *opportunity*
of, like,
*forty lifetimes*,"
        Mom insisted.
"You'll learn
        so much
        from Terrance.

He already
knows about
and cares about
        *you*.

He knows what
we went through
with Dad."

My head
was a stinging
        swirl
                of hornets.

For days
after the letter came,
        I gave Mom
        every reason
        I could think of
        not to move.

*You can do*
*your exercises*
*here.*
        *You don't need*
        *to leave home*
        *to learn how*
        *to breathe.*

*And can't you*
*stretch*
*and do yoga*
*at the gym?*
        *The type of yoga*
        *Terrance does*
        *isn't even*
        *real.*

*And why does it matter*
*if the Center*
*has a garden?*
        *We have*
        *our own garden.*

I looked up
everything I could
about groups
like Helioras.

One article
I found
asked:
        IS HELIORAS
        A CULT?

It mentioned
other
known cults.

I Googled
their names.

        Branch Davidians.
            The Peoples Temple.
                Heaven's Gate.

I showed Mom
the findings
on my phone.

"If Terrance
is running
a cult,
he might try
to kill us,"
        I suggested.
"Or make us
        kill ourselves."

I pointed to
a web page.

"In Waco, Texas,
the Branch Davidians
were hardcore
Bible people.

They believed
their leader
was a prophet
of the End Times.

> There was
> a long standoff
> with the FBI.
> In the end,
> most of the Branch Davidians
> *were burned alive.*

Even the
kids."

"I remember
watching
the fire at Waco
on TV,"
> Mom said.
"This isn't
like that.

> Terrance
> is *not*
> a Bible person."

"What about
Jonestown?"
        I asked.
"That's where
the phrase
*Don't drink
the Kool-Aid*
comes from.

        The Peoples Temple
        Jim Jones led
        started out
        great.

It was about
equality
for all people.

        They built a community
        in Guyana
        for everybody.
        Jonestown was
        a jungle paradise.
        With *gardens.*
        And little cabins.

But Temple members
murdered a Congressman
and reporters
who came to visit.
They knew
they couldn't
get away
        with the killings.

So Jim Jones
made everyone
kill *themselves.*"

I pulled up
images from Google.

"Even the kids
had to drink
the poisoned Kool-Aid,"
I told Mom.

"Jim Jones
was a communist,"
said Mom.
"And he was
leading a religion.

Terrance
isn't political
*or* religious."

"But they wear jumpsuits
at the Healing Center,"
I said.

"Have you heard of
Heaven's Gate?"

"I'm not sure,"
Mom sighed.

"When that group
killed themselves,
they all wore
purple jumpsuits,"
     I told her.
"The patch
on the suits said:
     *Heaven's Gate Away Team.*

     They drank
     a toxic mix
     as the Hale-Bopp comet
     flew over them.

They thought
after they died,
they would
wake up
inside of a spaceship."

"Look."
     Mom sighed
     again.
"That doesn't
sound *close*
to what Terrance
believes.

     You know
     better."

"I read about
some creepy
California cults
too,"
        I added.
"Like the Manson Family
        and
        the Source Family
                and
                the Buddhafield.

        I think you –"

"Stop-stop-stop!"
        Mom's
        shout
        tore into me.
"You need to
*get rid*
of that
ugly fear
and worry
        inside of you,"
        she said.
"Terrance helps
with that.

He doesn't
want anyone
to kill or die.

        He wants
        them to have
        *new life.*"

So it was
settled.
No more
excuses.

We would
leave our home
as quickly
as Terrance
      asked us to.

      Mom had
      already left
      her job
      as a bank manager
      in Palo Alto
      months ago.

We had enough
money
from Dad's
life insurance.

      And Mark said
      we'd have
      more support soon.
      Our lawsuit
      over Dad's
      wrongful death
      was making
      progress.

Ms. Hernández,
the teacher
in charge of
Chess Club,
cried
when she heard
I was leaving.

"Be strong,
Maggie,"
　　　she said,
　　　struggling
　　　to yank
　　　a tissue
　　　from its box.
"Be there
for your mother
when she
needs it."

"Don't worry,"
　　　I said,
　　　holding
　　　the box
　　　for her.
"I'll be
　　　watching out
　　　for whatever
　　　game
　　　is going on
　　　at Helioras."

And soon,
so soon,
we were
        snaking
        along
        Route 101.

Mark drove,
        one hand
        at the wheel.
Mom gripped
        his other hand.

We'd left most
of our things
                behind.
Locked away
        in closets.

The home
        itself was
        rented out
to tourists.

Strangers
        who'd sleep
in my bed.
        Faces
I'd never
        know.

In a year,
        would I even know
        my own face?

On the ride,
we didn't
        listen to
                a single song.
Even when
        Mom wanted
to turn
the radio on.

Mark told her
to focus on
        what was ahead.

So it was all
        podcasts.
All Terrance.
        Hour
        after
        hour.

Terrance was
the voice of time.
The shedding
skin
of the *now*.

Time
and the road
        snaking
        on.
Like
        twin serpents
underneath
        a blazing sun.

# TOUR

The Helioras Healing Center
is enormous.

Its windows
are tidal waves.
They carve
the sides
of the Center
into white petals.
Like the famous
Opera House
in Sydney –
the Australian city
where Terrance
is from.

When you enter
the lobby,
a giant medallion
looms over you.
The Helioras logo
with the two snakes.

Smiling people
greet you with hugs.
When you speak,
they always
keep eye contact.

You might
notice their
dull gray jumpsuits.
If you ask
about them,
they'll say
it reminds them
    how the spark
    is in
    each of us.

    Not in the
    material world.

The world
of clothes
and cars
and cash.

    The world
    of pollution
    and pills
    and paranoia.

That world
is gray.

    Our source
        is
    *bright.*

Then they might
unzip
the tops
of their jumpsuits.

Just enough
to show you
the burning yellow
along the
inner flaps.

The brightness
hidden
within.

They'll
take you onto
the peacock carpet
in the Enlightenment Hall.

A welcome video
from Terrance
will play.
Another clip will
walk you through
some basic exercises.

Do them.

The exercises *will*
        make you feel
                more alert
                        and alive.

Afterward,
you'll eat
the best vegan food
you've ever had
in the Next Life Dining Hall.

Most of the food
is grown
in the Center's
World Soul Garden.

Mixed melons.
Cabbage,
         carrots,
                  cauliflower.

Once you've
had your fill,
you can tour
the bedrooms.

Each of the spaces
includes two bunks
and a TV.

The TVs
mostly stream
Terrance's daily broadcasts.
They also have a
digital library of
Terrance's older talks
and exercise videos.

         No other channels.

Guides won't let you
into the Control Room
where Terrance
does his broadcasts.

And they won't
even tell you about
the Growth Room.

You might see
a white door
marked by
a single
golden leaf.

If you ask about it,
your guides
will say
it's for supplies.

You might not
believe them.

You might
want to know
        what's behind          such a strangely
marked
        door.

If somehow
you did steal
a set of keys,
        you could
        open it.

You could learn
what Helioras
is hiding.
Beneath all
the hugs
          and smiles
and fresh foods
          and deep breaths.

Turn the knob
          and see
                    the truth.

Light
will throw itself
into the
narrow space.

And that's when
you'll be
disappointed.

By four walls with
beige soundproof panels.
A simple
sun mosaic
on the floor.

          There's
          nothing
          else
          inside.

# HAIR

Of course,
one day,
I was there
inside the Growth Room.
    Trapped
    in darkness.

When Terrance
    threw me in,
    it was for
    my own good.

To seal off
the negative energy
I brought.
To keep us all
on a better path.

I'd only been
at Helioras
for three months
when I decided
to send
my dangerous email.

I couldn't
have done it
without Chinara.

Chinara
was my newest friend.
We did schoolwork
together
in the Next Life Dining Hall.

She had come from
Nigeria
with her father,
who was
hired by a
San Francisco startup.
He had learned
about Helioras
from one of
his coworkers.

Chinara's mother
remained
in Nigeria.
She was taking
care of
Chinara's grandmother,
who was sick
with tuberculosis.

Chinara told me
she wanted to
become a doctor.
To return to her country
and help people
like her grandmother.

But for now
she sat
across from me
in "school."

On the day
I asked for Chinara's help,
we were working
on essays about
Enlightenment thinkers.

Ms. Droghan,
our frizzy-haired "teacher"
at Helioras,
thought it was
a waste of time.

She told us
we only read
about
the so-called "Enlightenment"
because the state
         made us.

She said
the "Enlightenment,"
from hundreds
of years ago,
was a false one.

         Pigheaded European men
         had terrible ideas
         about science
         and government.

These ideas
only led
to bloodshed
        and suffering.

Ms. Droghan
told us about
the French Revolution.
The revolutionaries
thought they found
"Enlightenment."
They thought
they knew
everything.
They even built
their own
Temple of Reason.

Soon enough,
they were
    chopping
    off
        each other's heads.

This wasn't
*real* Enlightenment.
The teachers
the revolutionaries
followed
were not wise.

They didn't
understand
spiritual truths.

Terrance studied
wiser teachers.
He knew
the full truth
of how the universe
really
worked.

We lived out
the amazing journey
        to *real* Enlightenment
        every time
        we did exercises
        on the peacock carpet.

Ms. Droghan
was sure of this.

And maybe
she was right.

The exercises
we did
and the meals
we ate
did make me
feel healthy.

Most of
Terrance's talks
were upbeat
and inspiring.

But I still
didn't trust
him.

My stomach
        felt tight
                and twisted
        when he
                spoke.

Chinara said
she usually
liked Terrance.
But she had
her doubts too.

"I remember
last month,
he told us how
        sleeping together
was a
waste of
creative energy,"
        Chinara
        whispered
        to me once.
"But we all
        know
he is
sleeping
with Lila."

I only saw
Terrance
in person
about once
a week.
But when he
appeared,
Lila,
as his assistant,
always stood
close beside him.

She liked
to kiss
his hands.
Run
her fingers
        through his hair.

When
she did this,
he smiled
        slyly.
Like they shared
        some dirty secret.

Lila beamed
her happiness
back into him.

Her eyes
were lit
with love.

This wasn't the reason
why I sent
my email though.

This wasn't why
I passed
a note
to Chinara.
When our
teacher wasn't
looking.
When she thought
I was
scribbling
something
on
the French Revolution.

My note
asked about
Mr. Ogbu's
laptop.

I passed it
because of what
Terrance had done
to my mom
the day before.

In the past,
he was always
kind to her.

He said she was
more than his
"spark of sunlight."

She was a
"beloved
servant of
the star
        within."

But the day before,
he walked
into the
World Soul Garden.

Mom was
in charge of
caring for
the garden's
tomatoes.

I was helping
water
the rows
when Terrance
arrived.
His hands
were pressed
        together.

He told Mom
the tomato rows
were
        crooked.

That meant
her heart
was
         crooked.

It meant
she was still
too concerned
about Dad's death.

She did not
care enough
about
finding light
*now.*

She needed
to fix this.
To prove
she wanted
true peace.

He told her that,
to heal herself
*now,*
she must
tear
out
a lock of hair.

When
he said this,
I
        dropped
my watering can.
        But didn't
        speak up.

Terrance
showed
the white
of his twinkling teeth.

He nodded
for me
to pick up
the can.

Then
returned
to Mom.

"Tear out
your hair,"
        he said
        patiently.
"With your
bare hands.

        Pull
        out
        the weakness
        in your body."

He pointed
to others
in the garden.
They watched
like gray statues.

"Show them
        you are more
                than just
                        your
                        body,"
                                he said.

Lila was standing
next to Terrance.
Grinning like
a schoolyard bully
        in a bad movie.

She bobbed
her head
in delight.

I wanted to
yell,
but I was
        frozen.
A gray statue
myself.

Mom bit
into her lip.

At first
it looked like
      she
      wasn't going
      to
      obey.

But then
she took off
her garden gloves.
Underneath,
her hands
were still caked
in soil.

She dug
both
of those
trembling hands
into the nest
of her hair.

Her nose
scrunched up.
Like when
she listened
very hard
to something.

She tried
not to scream
as her nails
      ripped
at her scalp.

Terrance squeezed
her shoulder
        gently
while she
        pulled.

"Pain is growth,"
        he whispered.

A thin trickle
        of blood
        ran
        down
        Mom's
        forehead.

"On the other side
is a better *now*,"
        he cooed.
"A *now*
        you deserve."

Mom
        tugged,
                tugged,
                        tugged.

                        A gray-black
                        patch
                        of hair,
                                matted
                                with red,
                        came out
                        in her palm.

Terrance carefully took
the bloody lock
from
Mom's hands.

> He placed it
> in the pocket
> of his jumpsuit.

His hands
> cupped
> her cheeks.

He peered
into her.
Sharing
the view
of the sea
his eyes held.

"Don't you
feel better?"
> he asked.
"Don't you
feel cleaner?
> And clearer?
More at home
with yourself?

There's so much
light and love
inside you.
I feel it *bursting*
through your bones."

I was
still frozen.

My heart
pumped out
a fear
that made
my muscles
fix
in place.

Terrance
bent in
to hug Mom.
And she wept
into his arms.

She cried,
          "Thank you,
                    thank you,
          thank you,
                    *thank you."*

Underneath the tears,
she was glowing.
Shining like
she had been
made new.

But I knew
I could not
let this
go.

My phone
was taken
from me
when I first
entered Helioras.

But I was aware
that Mr. Ogbu
was one of a few people
allowed a computer
for his work.

He let Chinara
use it sometimes.
To video chat
her mom.
To check in
on old friends.
She even had
his password.

I could
send out
a signal
to save us.
Contact
the media.
Tell them
my story.
Before Terrance
did something
         even more
         terrible.

I threw my
question to Chinara
using a torn
piece of notebook paper.

She gave
a worried glance
as she read my note.
       But then
       she flipped it over.
Wrote a single word
on the back.
       Crumpled up
       my sheet.
Dropped
the note on the floor.
       Kicked it
       under the table.

I reached down
when others
weren't looking.
Uncrumpled
the paper.

Just opening
the sheet
felt like Enlightenment.

My path
forward
was written within:

       *SunSPARKhealer181*

# LUNGS

I still remember
       how dizzying
              it was.

       The rush
       of release.

My fingers
       tingling
               with electricity.

Mr. Ogbu
would be back
from his exercises
at any moment.
Time
ticked
in my throat.

I pressed
SEND
on the email.

Shot my message to
       four different reporters
       I'd found online.
       People covering stories
       in the San Francisco Bay Area
              and beyond.

Now they'd know
about me
and my mother.

They'd
care about us.

Tell our
story.

Put a
stop
to Terrance.

That was
the dream,
at least.

Of course,
it never
happened
that way.

As far as I know,
only one
reporter
even dialed up
Helioras.

Terrance must have
tricked the caller.

With his candy-coated
words.

Who knows
what he said.

    Who knows
    how he won
    the reporter
        over.

But
I know now
he
cannot
be
crossed.

Last night,
he plucked me
out
of a Friday energy circle.
A dozen of us
were holding
hands.

Chinara's hand
was in mine.
My hand
was in Mom's.
Mom's hand
was in Mark's.
And Mark's hand
was in Lila's.

We were taking
     quick       breaths
         through our noses.

*in     in     in     in     in*
   *out   out   out   out   out*

Slower now.

     Through
     the mouth.

*Iiinnn       iiinnn*
    *ooouuut     ooouuut*

Breath
is
energy.

Breath
is
life.

Breath
is
*now.*

Feel
the miracle
that you are.

*in    in    iiinnn     in    in    iii–*
  *out   out    ooouuut   out   out*

Terrance
      grabbed
          the air
          from my lungs.
With two hands
      on my
shoulders.

He    sp    lit
      the circle    apart.

    I
      tumbled
        back
    onto
      the carpet.

Terrance      waved    to Lila.

She grabbed
    my ankles.

Terrance gripped my arms
      and they l i f t e d  me.

    The
      seconds
        seemed
     to spin
   around
      themselves.

And Mom didn't even question this.
She just kept breeeeaaathing.
      *Ouuuuuuutttttt..................*

When I wiggled,                    a hammock.

                    I                    like

                              swung

My
          body
                    was a swaying
          net
                    that caught
          the world
                              inside it.
                    Snatched the eyes
                         of the stars.

My                              the hand of
          neck              like                    a clock.
                    turned

And I saw
the              mystery door
                         swing          back.

The Growth Room
     opened

          wide.

          To breathe
                    me

               in.

The long
throat
of a

serpent.

The deep
lungs
of the

darkness.

You'll
        *spin*
*down,*
        *down*
        *into*
        *a*
        *bottomless*
        *well.*

I was begging
        Terrance,
            Lila,
                Mom,
                    God,
"Please-what-no-what-are-you-what-are-please-"

Down.
Set
down.
In the shadow sun
on the
dimmest floor.

*You'll slip*
*away*
*from everyone.*

"Don't lock
      me in!"
I screamed,
      fighting
      to stay
      with the light.
      "Don't lock me in.
            Don't lock me.
                Don't lock me
                *in the dark* —"

"Dark?"
      Terrance's voice
      was a flat sneer.
"This isn't
      the darkness.

You are
      the darkness.
You are
      the host
      of your own
      hell.

And we can't
have
hell
here,
      can
      we?"

Lila's eyes
were bright
and playful.

She kissed
Terrance's palm.

Before the sliver
        of light
                became thin.

Before
        the door            shut.

Before
        the lock
                clicked.

And
I shivered
alone
in
the soundless
void.

I placed my head
on the freezing tiles.
To remind myself
the room

was solid.

I
curled
up
inside
my panicked breaths.

I
could not
slow them.

I
could only
feel the
moment
pulse
invisibly
          through me.

My mind
          flowed          out

                    into     the
                                   black.

*You have*
*no control*
*over this.*

          *No control*
          *at all.*

NOW
PRESENTING:

# THE PRESENT

# RETURN

Peacock carpet.

Eyes of
the stars.

I am
here *now*.

In this
room.

Where we
are supposed
to find Enlightenment.

Chinara
is still
slumping.
Staring at
the floor.

Mom is
hugging
Mr. Ogbu.

And I
do not know
what to say
or think.

I have come
out of the darkness.
Into a light
that makes
no
sense.

My body
swims
over to
Chinara.
And I
whisper,
        "I'm sorry.
                I hope
                Terrance
                didn't do anything
                weird
                to you
                or your dad."

"I don't want
to talk about it,"
        Chinara says,
        eyes sunken.
"We just have
to trust
the system,
        you know?

        What other hope
        do we have?"

"Maybe
our hope
is away
from here,"
        I whisper.
"I can't let him
break us.
        I can't."

"You haven't
learned anything."
        Chinara sighs,
        then glances
                at me.
"But I'm
almost grateful
for that.

        Almost."

We move out
of the
Enlightenment Hall.
Toward the
bedrooms.
If the others
see us go,
they pretend not to.
They keep
to their conversations.

        They do
        not follow.

"You want
to know
what Terrance
did?"
        Chinara asks
        when we turn
        the corner.
"He's
not letting us
speak to Mom
for one week.
And I cannot
chat
with my friends
ever again.

That's what
came from
your genius plan."

"I'm sorry,"
        I say.
"I thought the reporters
would care more,
        I guess."

"They have
to make sure
a story is true
before they write it up,"
        says Chinara.
"And how would
they do that
        with what you told them?"

"We're just being
outplayed,"
        I say.
"This is like some
crazy chess game.

Terrance is the king.
        Lila is his queen.
Mark is a bishop
        or a knight.
                I'm not sure."

"And we're pawns,"
        Chinara says,
        finishing my thought.
"I get it,
        I get it."

I nod and say,
"The important thing
is to get away
from the
entire grid.

To flip
        the game
                over.

We don't
have to
play it."

Chinara
leans
against the wall.

Looks up
at the ceiling.

"There are
worse games,
you know,"
she says.
"There's
real evil
in the world.
War, famine,
addiction,
disease."

"Sure, but Helioras
is all twisted —"
I start
to explain.

"Even if
it's twisted,
it helps my dad,"
Chinara points
toward
the Enlightenment Hall.
"It gives him
peace."

"It gives
my mom
some fake peace
        too,"
        I spit.
"But it's
abusive.
        It's cruel.
                And it's wrong.

And it's only going
        to get
        worse.

If we don't
destroy
the game board,
        Terrance might.

He's playing
this whole game
against himself.

He can never
really win.
Or really lose.

And one day,
in frustration,
        he might
        murder
        us."

"We'll find
a way out
of this,"
      Chinara says.
"But you
*have*
to keep
your head.

Please try
to do that."

She laughs
a little
then.

"Terrance was wrong.
Obviously.

Throwing you
in that closet
didn't make
      you grow
      into his beliefs.

      But he is
      *s c r a m b l i n g*
      you.

You've been
rushing
too much
with your plans."

"You're probably right,"
            I admit.
"I think I need
        to lie down.
                That's all.
                        That's it..."

I feel
sleepy
suddenly.
Don't know
how much
        I slept.

My forehead
                pounds.

In sleep,
        I'll forget
about
the game.

Forget
that I'm here
in this body.
In this life.

Maybe a coma
is a beautiful rest.

Dad didn't
want to
come back
to us.

I let myself
drift away
from my friend.

I fall
onto the
starchy sheets
of my bed.

I didn't even
say goodbye
to Chinara.

I just floated
past her.
A loveless
ghost.

The more
Terrance talks
about love,
  the more
  I don't
  love anything.

The more
Terrance talks
about joy,
  the more
  it seems
  like a sick tease.

And if he takes
my love
and my joy,
does that mean
he's taken *me*?

Maybe
those things
died with Dad.

Maybe
I would give
my life
to Terrance
if what he said
were true.

That's why
Mom has to
believe.

She would
tear
out
all
her hair
just to live
in love.

But what kind
of love
works
that way?

# DEATHLOVE

*Unscramble.*

The TV
goes on
    by itself.

    Starts playing
        by itself.

        Starts talking
            by itself.

    This isn't
    a dream.

I'm coming up
        from the fog.
            Back to
                the bare bedroom.

    Terrance
    on the screen.

    One of his
    old broadcasts:
        "There is
        nothing to fear.
        So why fear
        nothing?"

I don't know
what he's talking
about.

I try to turn
the TV off,
        but it won't let me.

It's Saturday.
I should be free.
        To sleep.
                To escape.

"In death,
every NOW,
past,
        present,
and
        future,
becomes

        ONE."

I try to
mute the screen.
But I can't
even lower
the volume.

                He won't let me
                sleep.

                He'll never let me
                sleep again.

"The two snakes
of SELF
        and WORLD
come together.

They swallow
        each other.
They melt
        into
        a single
        brilliant sun."

                *What does*
                *that even mean?*

I just want
to sleep,
        want
                to sleep.

"I am here
        to guide you.

Through
the death
of SELF.

Through
the death
of WORLD.

        Into the
        light
        of PURE LOVE."

I throw
a bedsheet
over TV Terrance.

It won't stop
the sound.

"NOW
backwards
     is WON.

     Through
     death
     you have
     WON NOW!

WON
plus ONE
is TWO.

     Like
     the TWO
     serpents.

These
words
and numbers
are all
signals
from our SOURCE.

Truth travels
     through
     *my* energy."

I stumble
out of the bedroom
        to escape
        the voice.

But it still
wants me.

Still
wants me
to believe
every

word

it

says.

        "And NOW
        in THIS LIFE,
        my sparks
        of sunlight,
        you MUST LOOOVE."

Mark and Lila
are pressed
together
at the end
of the hall.

Tongues in
each other's
        throats.

Their
kisses
are wild.

      Hungry.

"LOVE on
each other's
bodies.

      LOVE on
      each other's
      souls.

LOVE,
      LOVE,
            LOVE."

The tongues
are two snakes.

      Trying
          to
               swallow
                    each other.

"Push out
the EVIL.

      Pull in
      the LIGHT."

Lila's open eyes
flash
as I pass her.

"YOU ARE
THE
SPIN            HEART
        NING
                OF EVERY
                        THING."

She bites
into Mark's neck.

        "LOVE

WHAT'S
                SPINNING
        OUT
                FROM
                        YOU!"

*Further.*

        *Further.*

Mark and Lila
fold behind me.
The rock gray
of their jumpsuits
        slides
                like an
        avalanche.

*Further.*

The glass doors
to the garden
are ahead.

"LOVE YOUR
        TEACHER."

Sunlight bathes
the courtyard.

"LOVE YOUR
        GUIDE."

I can see
Mom
bent over
her tomatoes.

Turning.

"LOVE YOUR
        SELF."

She opens
her arms.

*Here.*

# POISON

I
am
      panting.

Barely
      thinking.

Mom
is
      blinking.

"Mark's
with Lila,"
      I mumble.
"They're in
the hallway.

      All over
      each other.

Knew
you couldn't
trust him.

      I mean,
      he's our lawyer.
      Wasn't even legal
      for him
      to date you."

Mom
        blinks again.
                Scrunches
                her nose.

"I know
about
Mark and Lila,"
        she says.
"And they're free
        to love
        as they wish.

They have
Terrance's
        blessing."

The shadow
of a bird
        soars over
        the garden rows.

"A month ago,
sex was a waste
of creative energy.
Now *this*?"
        I ask.
"It doesn't hurt
for Mark
to do that?"

"Yes, it hurts,"
        Mom says,
        squinting.

"So why
are you
letting
it go?"
        I ask.

The wind
blows
a gray hair
onto Mom's nose.

"Pain
is growth,"
        she says.
"I hoped
you were learning
        that.

Terrance is trying
to help you
        get over
        yourself."

I don't
want
to fight her.

        I don't
        want
        to make a scene.

I'll get thrown
back in
the Growth Room.

"What would
Dad
think
of this?"
      I ask
      with a whimper.

"I don't know,"
      Mom says, frowning.
"He's on
      the other side
      of life.
We'll join
      him
      soon enough."

"What does
*that* mean?"
      I ask,
      chest clenching.

"We'll all
be joined
together again.
At a higher level.
When the
universe is
ready,"
      Mom says.
"We're
being burned
of our evil.
So the next world
      accepts us."

"But *how*
*do you know*
*that?*"
          I cry.
"And how
do you know
          Terrance
          will
          heal
          you?"

"My heart
knows,"
          Mom says,
          turning toward
          the tomatoes.
"How can I
          deny
          my heart?"

"By using your head,"
          I half-shout.
"Everybody thinks
          they're right
          about everything.

          But lots of people
                    are wrong."

Mom runs
          her gloves
          over the leaves
          of a tomato plant.

"Your negative energy

is bad
for me,"
          she says.
"I think
you should
          go away now."

"No, please,
let me stay,"
          I beg.
"Let me help
          with the garden."

Mom doesn't
face me.

The shadow
of another bird
flies over
her waving hair.

I cringe
at the memory
of her tearing
that precious hair
          out.

In this same
place.

Mom
reaches
into her pocket.

"Fine.
Get me
a bag of fertilizer
from the
supply closet,"
        she says,
        tossing me
        a set of keys.
"I need to
side-dress
the rows."

"Thanks,"
        I say.

She nods
absently.

"You can use
the silver one."

As I turn
to go,
she releases
a heavy breath.

        Looks around
        the garden.

Two gardeners
just left.
No one else
remains
but us.

"I *do* miss Dad,"
      she sighs.
"Sometimes
      I do wish
      I was
      *dead*."

More shadows
of birds.
More wind
howling
through
us.

I want to
embrace her.
To show her
I love her.
In more than
some questionable
"Terrance way."

      But I don't
      say anything.

I pass
through
the glass doors.

      Let her
      vanish
      from
      my sight.

Terrance's voice
still winds
its way
        down the halls.

"I SEND YOU
            WAVES OF JOY!
        FEEL THEM,
FEEL THEM!
                SHED YOUR FEAR!
        BASK IN THE
                DEATHLESS LIGHT!"

Will the
broadcasts
ever
end?

Terrance
won't
stop
until he has me.

Until I say:

        Yes,
                *I am*
                *no longer*
                *afraid.*

        *I am*
        *at one*
        *with*
        *myself.*

You've cured
my sickness.
By raising
the fever.
By burning
me up.

You can keep
the ashes.
Take my
leftovers.

That's when
I'll be cured
of my "evil."
When I won't be
anything
at all.

The silver key
meets
the grooves
in the
doorknob.

Turn,
        turn.

This closet
is not
a Growth Room.

It's not
empty.

I see
stuffed
shelves.

Boxes,
        bags,
barrels.

So many
labels
to read.

Pest and
        weed control.

Bleach and
        ammonia.

Some of
the cartons
and bins
have stickers
with skulls
on them.
Phone numbers
for Poison Control.

In the hall
behind me,
Terrance's broadcast
mentions
DEATH
        three times.

*Why?*
Why keep
toxic chemicals?

Shouldn't
everything
at Helioras
be organic?

In my mind's eye,
I try to picture
a peaceful future.

Ocean breezes.
Sandy beaches.
Happy creatures.

Instead,
I see Jim Jones
calling to his followers.
Telling them
to lay down
their lives.
To let
the little ones
take
the poison first.

I see the *Heaven's Gate Away Team*
stretched out
in their jumpsuits.

The skulls
on the stickers
are smiling.

The same
unknowing smile
        of those
            who follow Terrance.

The deadly ingredients
        are all
                here.

In the
supply closet.

Waiting to
end
the Helioras game.

To flip
        the board.

Is Terrance
already tired
of playing
with
everyone?

        Am
        I
        just
        tired?

The
closet
crowds
around
me.

An empty closet
      is for
      GROWTH.

A full closet
      is for
      DEATH.

WHY?

Break
      ing
                  my
      c l
      u t t e
      r e d
      mind.

So is
      my mind
the
      poison?

The     disease?

Is that
      the
      lesson?

*Wrong.*

All
     wrong.

Terrance
is going to
kill us.

One way
or another
I'm sure,

he

is

going

to

kill

us

all.

# KEYS

On my
mother's
key ring,
there are other
keys.
To other
doors.

These keys
are in
my hands.
But I don't know
what
they're for.

What else
does Terrance
trust my mother with?

I grab
a crumpled bag
of fertilizer
from
the closet.
Switch
off the lights.
Leave the
smiling skulls
          to the darkness.

Terrance's
broadcast
has finally
stopped.

I flop
the fertilizer
against
the wall.
Walk through
silent halls.

Step over
the eyes of
the stars.

Face the
door with
the golden leaf.
Test the
keys on
the Growth Room.

One key
makes
the knob move.
I pull it out
quickly.

I don't want
to look inside
again.

I head
toward
the lobby.
Pass
a fire extinguisher.

The Control Room
is on my left.
There is
an open palm
with an eye
in its center
on the door.

A bronze key
allows me
to turn the knob.

I let myself
glance inside.
See the shapes
of monitors.
Switches
and screens.

I shut
the door.

I don't know
how many
hidden cameras
are in the Center.

Pocketing
the keys,
I head back
to where I left
the fertilizer bag.

This time,
the halls
are not silent.
I see Ms. Droghan
ahead.

"I loved
your paper
on the
French Revolution,"
        she says
            in passing.

I give her
a polite nod
as she
floats away.

                *Just wait*
                *until*
                *I cut off*
                *your king's*
                *head.*

                *Then there'll be*
                *a real*
                *revolution.*

I lift
the bagged fertilizer
from the floor.

Go back
through
the glass doors.

Return to
the garden.

"What
took you
so long?"
Mom asks.

She looks
too tired
to care
about my answer.

"I don't know
how you can
find anything
in that closet,"
I say,
handing her
the keys.

She puts them
back
in the pocket
of her jumpsuit.

"Do you know
how to dress
the rows
with fertilizer?"
        she asks.

"No,"
        I say.
"But you can
teach me."

As I try
to follow
her directions,
I feel around
my own pockets.

        Brush my fingers
        along
        the teeth
        of metal grooves.

I hope Mom
doesn't notice.

If she
checked
her set of keys,
she just might notice
that the bronze one
        is
        missing.

# IMPULSE

"I'm sorry
it's short notice,"
     I say.
"I know
I'm insane."

"Do you
want us
both
to get locked up?"
     Chinara asks,
     as we sit together
     on her bed.
"You're
being
*impulsive*."

"Yes,"
     I agree.
"But I saw
the chemicals.
     I saw the
     skull stickers.
          And we both
          know
          this *is*
          a cult."

"Most cults
don't end
in suicide
or
murder,"
      she says.
"You don't even
have
a real plan.

When
Terrance catches up
to us,
what will
his next punishment
be?

Will I be
banned
from speaking
with my mom
*for good?*"

"Look,
I have
a real plan,"
      I insist.
"If everyone
knows
about the poisons,
      they'll wake up.

      See how endangered
      they are."

Chinara
holds her fist
against
her lips.

"You're wrong
about this,"
        she says.
"You think
everyone else
is wrong
about everything.

        But sometimes,
        you're wrong
                too.

People aren't
going to react
the way
you think.

        And you can't
        control
        what they'll do."

"But I can
tell them
the truth,"
        I say.
"Help me
do a broadcast.

        Please."

"How would
I even know
how to use
the equipment?"
        Chinara asks.

"We'll mess around
until we
figure it out,"
        I tell her.
"That's what
my dad
told me
to do.

When I was fourteen,
he took me
to a parking lot.
At a community college.

There weren't
many cars there.
So he said
to get behind
the wheel.
Figure out
which pedal
makes you go.
Which one
makes you brake.

        Figure it out
        yourself."

Chinara
looks up
at the ceiling.
Just like
she did
in the hall.

Earlier today.

*How
is it
the same day?*

*Time is
        broken,
broken.*

"If you can
figure it out
alone,
        then why
        do you
        need me?"
        she asks.

Her eyes
are wide
and searching.

I lean
into her ear.

I whisper
my reply.

# AFTER

Saturday night.

After
a dinner of
kale and apple salad.

After
banana bread
for dessert.

After
we lie down
in the Enlightenment Hall.
Face up
on tie-dye towels.
Hands at our sides.
Breathing in
uneven patterns
until we
disappear.
Our breaths are
so shallow,
we
pass
out.

After we've
woken.
Sobbing.
Twitching.
Barely aware
of the world
crackling
around us.

After Lila
leads us
through
comedown
exercises.

After we're treated
to an extra
broadcast
from Terrance.

After he
sends us
good vibrations.
Bows to
the sun
shining
in our hearts.

After we've
hugged
and kissed
each other
goodnight.

After we
return to
our rooms.
Tuck ourselves
into starchy sheets.
Reflect
on the day
as it dies.

After every light
in the building
goes out.
Like a spirit
leaving
a body.
Like some
mindless machine
shutting
down.

After the moon
streaks through
the blinds.
Slices up
the tiles
into bars.
Fades
with the
crossing clouds.

After I hear
Mom's snores.
Charging
forward.
Clopping along
in sharp snorts.
So strange
and imperfect,
I feel
a sudden
happiness.

A sudden
calm.

After
all of this,
I rise.

Crack open
my
door.

It squeaks
slightly.
But the
snorting
continues.

And so does
the
movement
of my
bare feet.

*Walk,*
   *walk.*

Forward.

I will
   break
   this
   world.

*Break,*
   *break.*

Forward.

Shake
   and
shatter
   everything.

# WELL

"I was
able
to look up
a few things,"
      Chinara
      whispers.

We are in
the Control Room.

No lights on.

The space
is invisible
and shapeless.

It could be
as small
as the Growth Room.
Or as large
as a galaxy.

"Your dad
didn't change
his password?"
      I ask.

"No,"
        Chinara says,
        voice
        cracking.
"He
still
trusts me."

"So you know
how to work
these cameras
and computers,
then?"
        I ask.

"I don't know
if I know.
We'll
find out
in a minute,"
        she murmurs.
"But I did
some research.

I didn't
        just
        plunge
        in
        without
        any thought."

I'm
not thinking.

     I know
     I'm
     not thinking.

I'm just
moving through
each moment.
Fumbling
to find
some hidden path
forward.
Another square
to slide into.

     Just like
     Mom.
     Just like
     everyone.

"Do you
think
we can
even get
the power on?"
     I ask.
"Or is the
whole building
on lockdown
until morning?
     I wonder −"

My question
answers
itself.

My eyelids
snap
down.
Block out
the sudden white.

> For a second,
> I think
> Terrance
> has found us.

But when
I've adjusted,
I see Chinara.
Standing tall
beside
a light switch.

"Here's
*Lights*,"
>    she says.
"*Camera's* next.
>    Then *Action*,
>    if we're lucky."

I follow
her over
to a monitor.
She boots up
the computer.

I notice
a cable
plugged into
the hard drive.

It slithers
from the computer
to a sleek black camera
in the middle
of the room.

The camera
is pointed
like an alien's ray gun
at a long desk.

      Behind the desk
      is a swivel chair,
      padded
      with leather.

          Behind the chair
          is the Helioras logo,
          printed
          over a map
          of the world.

Chinara
taps on
a keyboard.

I think I see
the logo's snakes
      begin to squirm.

They wind
        their way
around
        the planet.

When
I blink,
they become
stable.

I'm
still tired.

Still without
any real sleep.

I try
to focus.

"Won't there be
another password
on that computer?"
        I ask.

"Probably,"
        Chinara says.

I'm grateful
she doesn't
refer again
to how little
I've been thinking.

I've rushed
      every part
      of this plan.

Hard to
believe
I ever was
a chess player.

That I ever was
patient.
      Calm.

A login prompt
      pops up
      on the screen.
To mock us.
To tell me
      how hopeless
      this is.

"Let's try
*password*
for the password,"
      Chinara says.

Of course,
this doesn't
work.

Terrance isn't
that dense.

"What about
your dad's password?"
        I ask.

Chinara types in
*SunSPARKhealer181.*

The screen
starts to load
a user's desktop.

"Perfect,"
        Chinara
        laughs.
"I think
that must be
the generic password
around here."

My skin
tingles
with excitement.

"This is
happening,"
        I say.
"This is
really happening."

"Could be."
        Chinara
        grins.

She explores
the desktop
once it's loaded.

I watch
her fingers
click and tap.
They remind me
of rain
on a rooftop.

*Like rain*
*that comes*
*during a*
*morning bike ride.*
*On a summer road.*
*With Dad.*

*He's much faster*
*than me.*
*His bicycle*
*has so many*
*speeds and gears.*
*But he coasts.*
*Lets me catch up.*

*The ride starts sunny.*
*But he points*
*at the clouds.*
*The gathering gray.*
*Rain pounds us*
*before we reach*
*the cabin we've rented*
*at a muddy campground.*

On the way back,
I wipe out
on the pavement.
Bend the frame
of my bicycle.

But Dad
helps me up.
Brushes
bits of rock
out of my shin.
Walks his bicycle
alongside mine
for almost a mile.
Rain soaks
through my shorts.
Washes out
my wound.

When we're finally back,
I shower
and change clothes.
Dad boils water in a pot
over a portable burner.
Then pours in
hot chocolate mix
from a tin.
He's also brought
a record player.
Puts on albums
from the '70s.
Music he says he loved
when he was a kid.

My shin pulses
under bandages
and ointment.
But I'm warm
and whole
as the rain raps
        on     on     on     on.

We play
Go Fish and Rummy.
Dad keeps
singing along
to songs I don't know.
Mom harmonizes
with him,
rubbing a blue crystal
at her neck.

I don't remember
the name
of the campground.
I don't remember
what specific songs
were playing.

I just remember
the feeling
of perfect trust.
I could take
any slip
or scrape.
Because in the end,
        all would
        be well.

"Hey,
        *Maggie.*
Hey,
                *Maggie!*"
Chinara
barks.

        Breaking
        the memory.

                Breaking
                the trance.

"I think
I've got it.

        You ready?

Let's get going,
get rolling,
and get out
of here.

If you
know
what
you want
to say,
                I think
                we can
                go
                LIVE."

# BROADCAST

I shiver
in the seat.
Press my
sweaty palms
on the desk's
surface.
Leave sticky prints
on the wood.

The camera's stare
is too bright,
like a naked light bulb.
I want shade
and cover.

But there is
        none.

I'm opening
myself
        to everyone.

"Do you want
a countdown?"
        Chinara asks.
She's only
a few feet away.
But it seems like
light-years.

"Just do it,"
    I say.
"Start
    the broadcast."

"You're about
to be
in every bedroom
in this building,"
    Chinara reminds me.

"Yes,"
    I say.
"*Please.*
Just do it.
    Crank it up.
        Blast me out."

"Okay,
    here we
    go."
    Chinara's voice
    lifts off.

THREE
    TWO
        ONE

A tiny bead
of red light
appears
above
the camera.

I
am
ON.

I
am
LIVE.

I
am
HERE.

"S-s-sorry
        to wake
        you.

I know
        we all need
        rest.

But I need
        you
        to hear something.

Something you
        should've,
                I hope,
                figured out.

Please
listen.

It's important."

A dry gulp.
I wish
I had a glass of water.

To take away
the tightness
in my throat.

The little red light
seems
like
it's
s
      p
              i
              n
              n
     i
n
      g.

"Terrance
is going
to poison us,"
      I tell
         the red light.
"There's
evidence
of this.

I've seen
the chemicals
he's going
to use.

Terrance–
he's like Jim Jones.

      You've all heard
      about Jim Jones.

Jim Jones
killed kids.

I m-m-mean,
he made
kids
drink poisoned Kool-Aid.

      But you
      know that.

I mean,
you do,
right?

      This is
      a death cult.

Terrance
talks about
death.
That's the last step
in his system.

      Because
      he's preparing us
      to die for him."

The red light
is a tunnel.
Sucking me
in.

"I think
he wants us
to die now.

          And he'll say
          it's peace and freedom.
                    Won't he?

          It's the best way
          to escape
          how evil and bad
          the world is.

It'll make us
one
with the universe.
Or something.

          But don't
          believe him.

          The universe
          didn't throw us
          in here
          just so we could
          throw ourselves      back out.

Right?"

Red light
　　　dividing.

Forming d o t s.

Tracking vital signs.... . . . .  .  .   .    .

Forming                    Grids,
squares.                   boards.

Pressing                   Back to
inward.                    the
                           t
                           u
                           n
                           n
                           e
                           l.

"M-maybe
we have to trust
we're all here
　　　for a reason.

But it's not
　　　for Terrance's reasons.

It's not
to get pushed
around as pawns.

His game
　　　is
　　　unwinnable."

Follow
      the
            tunnel.

Snaking
         into
         forked paths.

"And if
you don't believe me,
look at the
cleaning and garden supplies.

So much more
        than we need
just for the garden.

Terrance
can slip them
        into our food.
Bake them
        in our banana bread.

He doesn't mean us
        well.
He doesn't want
        to help –"

A far-off door
swings open.
Swats away
        the red light.

I see
the pale shape
of the
Reaper.

Lunging
after me.

      Chinara
      dives
      below
      a table.

Terrance
reaches
for my collar.
With
bumpy,
bony hands.

The seaside windows
of his eyes
show
tidal
      waves.

A senseless
storm.

      Raging.

No calm.
No control.

# UNTRUE

I'm
flung
aside.

Watching
Terrance
turn

to face
the red light
himself.

Like
Death
looking
into a mirror.

Turning itself
inside out.

"Go back
to sleep,"
          he says.
"This girl
doesn't know
          what
she's talking about."

"Why
would I
kill
a spark
of sunlight?"
　　　he asks
　　　the camera.
"Why
would I
do that?

　　　Anyone
　　　who works
　　　in the garden
　　　knows about
　　　the chemicals.

We're working
on getting
more natural
products.

　　　But for now,
　　　we're using
　　　what's cheap
　　　and effective."

"Everything here's
*cheap*
*and effective,*"
　　　I mumble.

"*Silence*,"
　　　he snarls.

"I want
Mark and Lila
at the Control Room,"
        Terrance tells
        the camera.
"We have two
young ones here
in need of
SO MUCH
GROWTH."

Chinara pokes
her head
        out,
then ducks
        back down.

"I apologize
for this
childishness,"
        Terrance
        continues.
"This is
very hurtful
for me
and for you.

Who knew
we had
this much
ignorance
and
hatred
        in our home?"

Lila
is at the door.

Mark
is behind her.

  Grim
  and gray.
  Like prison guards
  ready to
  throw me in
  solitary confinement.

"Come,
  love,"
  Lila calls.
"This doesn't
  need
  to be bad."

"We care
about you
very much,"
  Mark sings.

So it's more
darkness
for me.

More raging,
restless
night.

No control
over this.
No control
at all.

Terrance sits
        stony
        and still.

His head
casts a shadow
over the map
of the world.

Lila takes
my shin.

I try to
kick,
        kick,
kick,
        but Mark grips
            my other leg.

I'm carried past
Chinara.
Her face is buried
in her knees.

A scream
splits
a space
beyond us.

Mr. Ogbu
is shouting
from
the hall.

Mark and Lila
drop
their hands.
Let me
fall.

They rush
to the door.
Into the
shouts.

I rise
from the floor.
Follow
their flight.

Feel a crackle
            spiral
                    through me.

        "QUICK,
                QUICK!

                SHE IS DYING!
                        SHE IS DYING!
                SHE IS DYING!

        QUICK,
                QUICK!"

# BURN

Mom
      is flailing
on
      the peacock carpet.

Her
      mouth
frothing.

Bubbles
      blooming
and
      bursting.
Floating
      in acid.

She
      coughs
      all
      over
      the eyes of the stars.

"Higher level,"
      she manages
      to spit.
"Clear me.
Burn me
      up."

"What
did
you
drink?"
I screech.
"We need
a phone.

Call
Poison Control.

Right now!"

Mr. Ogbu
moves to get
his cell phone
from his room.

But Mark
grabs
his shoulder.

"Ssshhh,"
he says.
"We don't know
what's going on.

Don't want
to draw
this kind
of attention.

Just get her
some water."

"Don't
*you care*
*about her*
*at all?!"*
      I scream.
"She's *dying*
      *here.*

She had
the keys
to the supplies.

She must've
drunk
something
in there.

      *She must've*
      *drunk*
      *something."*

"You put
the thought
in her head,"
      Lila hisses.
"You did this
to your
mother.

She wanted
to serve Terrance.

You gave her
      the wrong instructions."

Was it
        *me?*

Did I
misunderstand
what the chemicals
meant?

And murder
my mother?

With
all the poison
        in my mind?

Oh, God,
*not my mom.*

        Give me
        a million years
        in the dark
        of a Growth Room.

A billion years
in the
deepest well
of the
deepest hell.

        But don't
        take Mom.

Take me,
        *take me.*

I see
all the demons
of the pit
circling around us.
An army
of gray.

Mark,
        Lila,
Ms. Droghan,
        Terrance.

*Terrance.*

"Leave us,"
        he tells me
        in a hollow tone.
"I want you *both*
        to leave.
I don't want you
or your energies here
        anymore.

The keys
to the company van
        are on
        your mum's chain.

        There's a hospital
        in Salinas.
        Follow the GPS
        on the dashboard.

        *Go!*"

I feel
a hazy glow
in my veins.

I
pull
Mom up.
As tremors
      spring
           through her body.

She spews
acid
onto my jumpsuit.

I almost
laugh.

Terrance
is setting
us free.

"Can
she even
drive?"
      Mark scoffs.

"My *dad*
taught
me,"
      I say.
"Help me
take your *girlfriend*
      to the van."

"You want
to go out
on *those roads*?"
        Mark asks,
        jaw set.
"With monsters
out there
like the
*drunken animal*
who killed
your father?"

"I'll take
my chances,"
        I say,
        as Mr. Ogbu
        helps balance Mom
        against me.
"I'll take
any chance
that isn't here."

"She *can't*
leave."
        Lila looks
        to Terrance.
"This is
a mistake.

        Think of
        the *lies*
        she's going
        to tell
        the press."

Lila's arms
     are vipers striking.
          Tearing me from my mother.

The woman
who gave me life
continues
     to vomit
     and shake.

I see
the fire extinguisher.
Hooked to the wall
     beside the Control Room.

I grab
the chilly canister.
Pull out the pin.
Point the hose
at Mark and Lila.

     *Spray.*

Lila
     shrieks.
Reaches
     for her
     eyes.
Mom
     twirls.

I hurl
     the canister
     into the crowd.

I catch
      Mom
before
      she
face-
      plants.

Drag her
      toward
            the exit.

Past the
      dimming sun.

Past the
      shriveling snakes.

Terrance
      shrinks
      into the mist
      behind me.

His shadow
      curves.

      Is he
      bowing?

I careen
      across the lobby.
            Through the front doors.
            Already unlocked.
            Somehow,
                  somehow.

Mom
       coughs
into
       the crisp
       night air.

The van
sparkles ahead.

The world
sparkles ahead.

The moon
and *real stars*,
with their
infinite eyes,
twinkle
around me.

"You'll need
a shower.
And hot chocolate.
And old music.
And Go Fish,"
       I tell my
       wilting mother.
"But you'll
be fine.

              I've got this
              under control."

       I don't know
       if she can even hear me.

# EMBRACING
# THE
# FUTURE

(One Last Exercise)

# MIND'S EYE

We'll be
at Stinson Beach.

Lying on
blankets.

Drinking in
every
spark
of sunlight.

Mom will
turn to me.
Nose scrunched.

"I'm so
grateful
to be here,"
        she'll say.
"To feel like
I'm
back together
again.

I'm so
sorry
for what
I did."

"It's okay,"
        I'll say,
        as waves
        strike
        the shoreline.

"I'm sorry
for trying
so hard
to control
how you felt
about things.

        Nothing
        turned out
        the way
        I thought
        it would."

Seagulls
might squawk.

I'll pat
Mom's arm
with a sandy hand.

"I can't
believe
I tried
to end *this*,"
        she'll say.
"What was
        I thinking?"

She'll put
her hand
over mine.

"I wanted
to please
Terrance,"
          she'll explain.
"But I didn't
owe
him
my life.

Thank God
that bleach
wasn't
enough
to kill me.

I'm sure
Dad's waiting for us
in the next world.
But he doesn't
need me
now.

*This world*
needs me
now.

You
need me
now."

At some point,
we'll pack up.
Head back
to our hotel.

Let the
sound of
the ocean
carry us on
through
all the life
we give
our attention to.

We'll climb
uphill.

Past the
giant rocks.
Whipped by
the waves.

Past towering palms.
Weeping willows.
Flowering trees
in full bloom.

Each perfect tree
was once
a simple seed.

In town,
we'll see
an elderly couple
playing chess
outside a worn café.

No matter
who wins the game,
they've both won
this shared *now*
together.

We'll spend
a *now*
buying ice-cream cones.
They'll drip
on our swimsuits
as we walk.

I don't know
what the old hotel
we arrive at
will be called.

But I imagine
it has a name like
The Serenity Inn.

When we reach
our room,
we'll take off
our sandals.
Turn up
the television.

There'll be
a news story on.

About Helioras.

We'll see
the Ogbus
on the screen.
Chinara
and her father.
Another woman
who must be
her mother.

They'll be
speaking into
an outstretched
microphone.

They'll be
telling
their story.

About
the pain.

     Violence.

     Manipulation.

And in
hearing them,
     I'll feel free.

No more
locked
chambers.

Repeating
broadcasts.

Unheard
screams.

They'll
            flutter
                                        off.

                        A dream
                          that
                         nearly
                        dissolves
                        when you
                          wake.

But
I will
remember
some
of the nightmare.

I will
be ready
to speak.

I'll write down
a phone number
for a tip hotline.

It'll race
through
the ticker
at the bottom
of the news story.

> I'll punch
> the digits
> into the
> landline phone
> at the side
> of my bed.

I'll take
a
long
breath
in.

Then
breathe out
into
the
handset.

I'll
say
everything.

# WANT TO KEEP READING?

If you liked this book, check out another book
from West 44 Books:

## *CLEAR CUT*
## BY MELODY DODDS

ISBN: 9781538385142

# SICK

They found Josie
in the locked bathroom
of a Bar Harbor café.

She had cut herself.

Her blood seeped
under the door.

I like to think
that it couldn't
        ever
have been me.

I would never be
            that careless,
                that sad,
                    that sick.

I *like*
to think that.

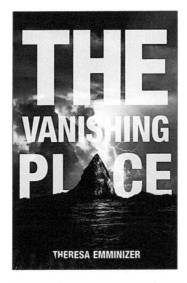

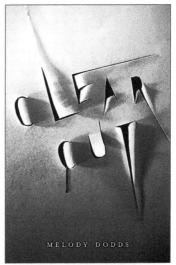

## CHECK OUT MORE BOOKS AT:
www.west44books.com

An imprint of Enslow Publishing

WEST **44** BOOKS™

# ABOUT THE AUTHOR

Ryan Wolf is the author of *Watches and Warnings*, a novel for young adults, as well as the Creepy Critter Keepers chapter book series for children. He has published stories, poems, essays, reviews, and journalism. Ryan holds his master's degree in the humanities from the University of Chicago. He lives in Oak Park, Illinois, with his wife, Jenna. Learn more about Ryan at www.ryanswolf.com.